Battle Day at Camp Delmont

NICKI WEISS

Battle Day

we welcome you to Camp Delmont

we're mighty glad you're here

the hills will be reverberating

with a mighty cheer

at Camp Delmont

PUFFIN BOOKS

we'll sing you in
we'll sing you out

for you we'll raise a mighty shout

hail, hail
the gang's all here

and you're
welcome to
Camp Delmont!

PUFFIN BOOKS
Published by the Penguin Group
Viking Penguin Inc., 40 West 23rd Street, New York, New York 10010, U.S.A.
Penguin Books Ltd, 27 Wrights Lane, London W8 5TZ England
Penguin Books Australia Ltd, Ringwood, Victoria, Australia
Penguin Books Canada Ltd, 2801 John Street, Markham, Ontario, Canada L3R 1B4
Penguin Books (N.Z.) Ltd, 182-190 Wairau Road, Auckland 10, New Zealand

Penguin Books Ltd, Registered Offices: Harmondsworth, Middlesex, England

First published in the United States of America by Greenwillow Books, 1985
Published in Puffin Books 1988
by arrangement with William Morrow and Company, Inc.
Copyright © Monica J. Weiss, 1985
All rights reserved

Library of Congress Cataloging in Publication Data
Weiss, Nicki.
Battle day at Camp Delmont/Nicki Weiss.
p.   cm.—(Picture puffins)
Reprint. Originally published: New York: Greenwillow Books, 1985.
Summary: While at camp together, Maude and Sally learn that they
can play competitively against each other and still be best friends.
ISBN 0-14-050761-2
(1. Friendship—Fiction. 2. Camps—Fiction.) I. Title. PZ7.W448145Bat 1988 (E)—dc 19 87-32724

Printed in Hong Kong by South China Printing Company

FOR LISA B.

Maude and Sally were best friends.

So when Sally said she was going back to Camp Delmont for another summer, Maude wanted to go too.

"Six weeks is a long time to be away, dear," Mama said.
"It'll be okay," said Maude. "I'll be with Sally."
"After all," Mama added, "it is your first summer at sleep-away camp."
"It'll be okay, Mama," said Maude. "Sally and I will be together."

And for the most part they were. They shared a bunk bed in their cabin, and Sally let Maude sleep on top since she had done that the summer before.

They took turns sweeping under the bed and straightening cubbies for inspection.

And when Sally had a stomachache and had to stay in the infirmary,

Maude pretended to have one because she wanted to stay there too.

On the canoe trip Sally steered because she had done that the summer before.

But at night by the campfire,
Maude was the one who was able to stuff the most marshmallows into her mouth.

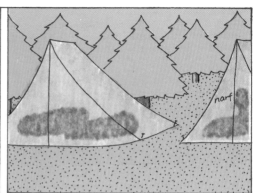

And when Berniece kept calling Fran a "narf,"
Sally went into their tent and sat on Berniece while Maude comforted Fran.
"It's only your name spelled backward," she said.

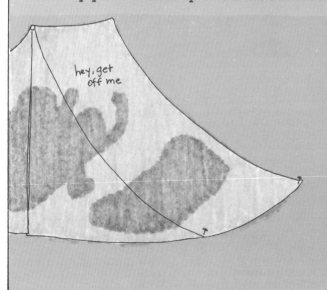

Maude didn't laugh when Sally got poison ivy between her toes.

Sally didn't laugh when Maude's bikini top slipped off while she was waterskiing.

And their counselor didn't laugh
when she caught them hopping around the bunk
in her pajama bottoms.

"Don't you two know how to do anything
without each other?" she asked.

And then, one day Maude wrote a letter home.

Dear Mama,

It's Battle Day at Camp Delmont tomorrow. We'll be split into the Red and White teams. I better be with Sally.
...day we went...it

The next afternoon the campers reached into a bag of buttons to see which team they were on.

Sally picked a red button.

Maude picked a white.

"Want to switch?" Maude asked Jessie,
who held a red button in her hand.
"I'll give you my white for your red," she said to Clare.

"There's no trading, Maude," said the counselor.
"But it won't be the same if I'm not together with Sally," Maude said.
"Sometimes you just can't be on the same side as your friends,"
 the counselor said. "You'll see. It will be okay to play against her."

she says
I can

now I have to
look for my
red shirt

But it wasn't okay.

When Sally fell in the three-legged race,
Maude reached down to help her up.

"Whose side are you on?" asked Sue,
who was tied to Maude.
"You almost pulled me down."

When Sally dropped her pail of berries
in the blueberry-picking contest,
Maude gave her some out of her own pail.

"I saw that," said Berniece.
"What do you think you're doing?"

When a ball was hit to the outfield in the softball game, Maude was so busy talking to Sally at second base that she forgot to run.

"You're on the White team, remember?" said Berniece. "You can only be on one team at a time," said Sue. "You can't be on both."

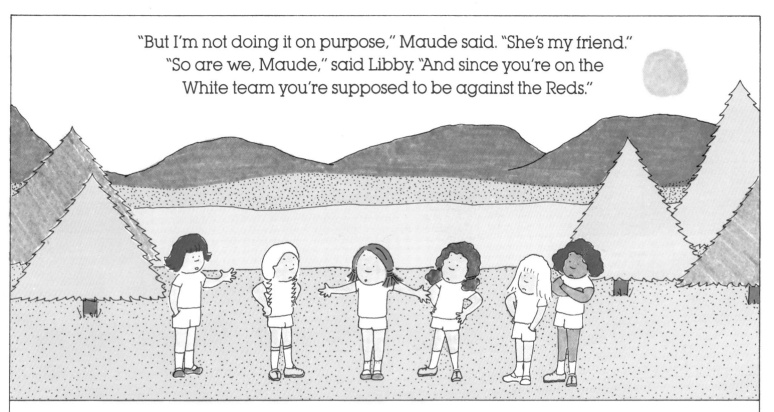

"But I'm not doing it on purpose," Maude said. "She's my friend."
"So are we, Maude," said Libby. "And since you're on the
White team you're supposed to be against the Reds."

Then they all headed toward the tennis court for the last game of Battle Day.

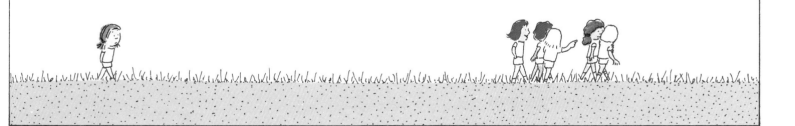

"Last two players in the game,"
the counselor shouted.
"It's Maude against Sally!"

Maude walked onto the court.
Sally served the ball.

Wham. Maude hit the ball.

Wham. Sally hit it back.

Wham. Maude hit the ball again.

And Sally missed it.

"We won! We won!"
shouted Libby as the campers
surrounded Maude.

"You were terrific," said Sally.
"That was really fun."

"At first we thought
you were on Sally's side,"
said Berniece.

"And then you won!" said Sue.

But even though the White team had won the tennis match, when all the points of all the games were added together, the Red team won Battle Day.

it's her name spelled backward

"Hey, Eceinreb," Fran called from her bed that night. "My team won."
"So?" said Berniece. "My team won last summer and will win again next summer."

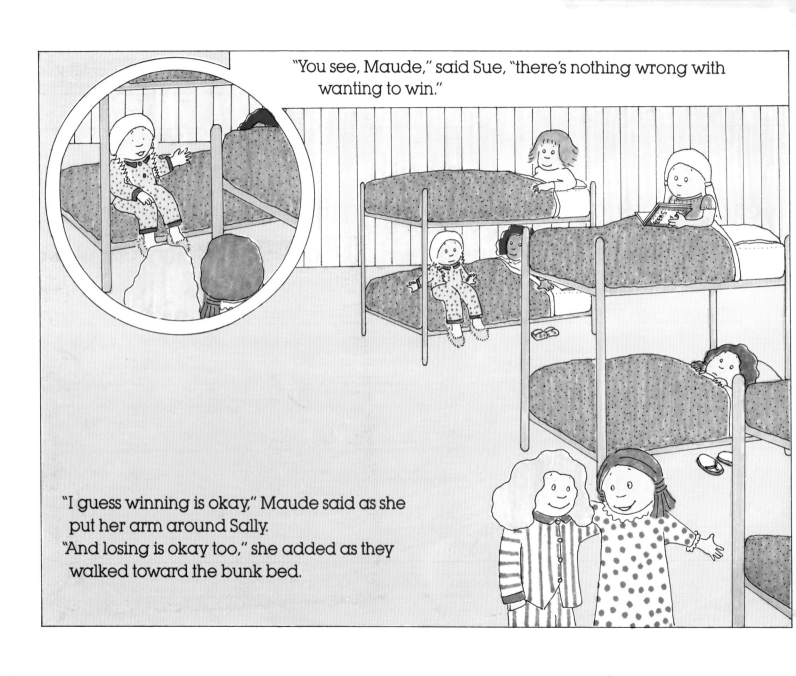

"You see, Maude," said Sue, "there's nothing wrong with wanting to win."

"I guess winning is okay," Maude said as she put her arm around Sally.
"And losing is okay too," she added as they walked toward the bunk bed.

Then the counselor came in to turn out the lights.

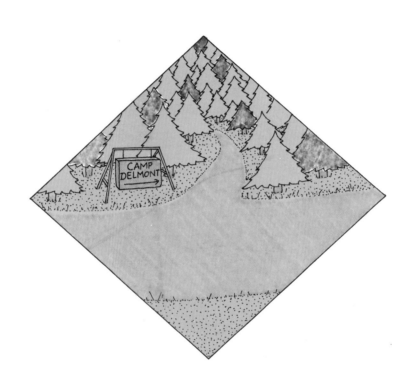